KT-458-379

The youngest was called David. He was small

and weak and liked to play music to the sheep.

One day, David's father had some bad news.

"Our land is at war," he told his sons.

"We must protect it. But I am too old to fight."

"I will fight," said Eliab.

"So will we!" said the other brothers.

"Me too!" David shouted.

"You are too small to fight, David," Eliab said.

"No, I'm not!" David said, standing up

as tall as he could.

"I need you to stay here and look after the sheep,

David," said his mother. "They will wander away

if no one watches them."

David watched sadly as his brothers marched off

to fight, and then he went to look after the sheep.

Chapter 2

All morning, David watched the sheep.

After a while, one of the sheep wandered off.

David fired a stone from his slingshot.

It landed near the sheep's feet with a PING!

"Baaa!" the sheep bleated, running back

to the flock. David was a good shot.

He knew he could help fight the enemy,

even though he was small.

At lunchtime, David's mother arrived

with a basket.

"Take this food to your brothers," she said.

"I will look after the sheep while you are gone."

David took the basket and began to run.

"Maybe when I get there, the army will let me

fight too," he thought, hopefully.

Chapter 3

When David reached the armies, they were stood
facing each other. He searched for his brothers.
He had never seen so many armed men.

David saw Eliab standing at the front.

"I brought your lunch," David told Eliab.

"Not now, David, we are getting ready to fight,"

Eliab said. "It is not safe for you here.

You must go now."

"But I want to help!" David insisted.

Suddenly, a giant man stepped forward from the enemy lines. David had never seen anyone so big. He wore golden armour that shone in the sun.

"My name is Goliath," he bellowed, "and I can stop this war. Our armies do not need to fight. Too many men will die. Choose one man to fight me instead. If he wins, then we will give you our land. But if I win, then you must give us your land."

15

"Who will fight Goliath?" David asked.

"Goliath is huge. Any man who fights him will be killed," Eliab argued. "Then we will lose anyway."

"Someone has to fight him," David insisted. "This is our chance to win without anyone else being hurt." Eliab and the other soldiers looked at each other, but no one spoke.

Chapter 4

Suddenly, David stepped forward.

"I will fight you, Goliath!" he cried.

"You?" Goliath said, peering down at David.

"But you are just a small boy."

"David, no!" Eliab cried. "Are you crazy?
You'll be killed!"

"Maybe I will," David replied. "But if I win,
hundreds of lives will be saved."

Goliath laughed. "You are the bravest boy I have ever met. I will even let you have the first shot!"

"Quick – give David your best armour

and weapons," Eliab told the soldiers.

But David shook his head.

"No, they are too big and heavy for me," he said.

He bent down and picked up five smooth stones

from the river. "These are all I need."

"Are you ready, Goliath?" David asked.

"I am!" he said, throwing back his head and roaring with laughter.

David fired a stone from his slingshot.

Everyone watched as the stone flew through the air ...

Chapter 5

… and hit Goliath right between the eyes.

Goliath crashed to the ground.

Goliath was dead. The enemy soldiers looked at him, then they looked at each other.

They all dropped their weapons and ran away.

27

"We won!" Eliab cried, lifting David

onto his shoulders and grinning.

David smiled. "I told you I wasn't too small

to fight."

"Hurray for David!" everyone cheered.

Things to think about

1. Why does David want to be allowed to fight?
2. Why do you think David's mother stops him fighting?
3. Why do you think Goliath challenges his enemy to fight him one to one?
4. How does David manage to beat Goliath, in your opinion?
5. This story has a lesson – what do you think the lesson might be?

Write it yourself

One of the themes in this story is bravery and belief in yourself. Can you write a story with a similar theme?

Plan your story before you begin to write it.
Start off with a story map:

• a beginning to introduce the characters and where your story is set (the setting);
• a problem which the main characters will need to fix;
• an ending where the problems are resolved.

Get writing! Try to use interesting noun phrases, such as "golden armour that shone in the sun", to describe your story world and excite your reader.

Notes for parents and carers

Independent reading
This series is designed to provide an opportunity for your child to read independently, for pleasure and enjoyment. These notes are written for you to help your child make the most of this book.

About the book
This is an exciting retelling of the famous story of David, a young shepherd boy, who bravely faces and defeats the mighty giant warrior, Goliath, armed only with a slingshot and pebble.

Before reading
Ask your child why they have selected this book. Look at the title and blurb together. What do they think it will be about? Do they think they will like it?

During reading
Encourage your child to read independently. If they get stuck on a word, remind them that they can sound it out in syllable chunks. They can also read on in the sentence and think about what would make sense.

After reading
Support comprehension and help your child think about the messages in the book that go beyond the story, using the questions on the page opposite. Give your child a chance to respond to the story, asking:

- Did you enjoy the story and why?
- Who was your favourite character?
- What was your favourite part?
- What did you expect to happen at the end?

Franklin Watts
First published in Great Britain in 2020
by The Watts Publishing Group

Copyright © The Watts Publishing Group 2020
All rights reserved.

Series Editors: Jackie Hamley and Melanie Palmer
Series Advisors: Dr Sue Bodman and Glen Franklin
Series Designers: Cathryn Gilbert and Peter Scoulding

A CIP catalogue record for this book is
available from the British Library.

ISBN 978 1 4451 7233 0 (hbk)
ISBN 978 1 4451 7238 5 (pbk)
ISBN 978 1 4451 7243 9 (library ebook)
ISBN 978 1 4451 7879 0 (ebook)

Printed in China

Franklin Watts
An imprint of
Hachette Children's Group
Part of The Watts Publishing Group
Carmelite House
50 Victoria Embankment
London EC4Y 0DZ

An Hachette UK Company
www.hachette.co.uk

www.reading-champion.co.uk

FSC
www.fsc.org
MIX
Paper from
responsible sources
FSC® C104740